ROY G. BIV and His Valuable Lesson

Hi, my name is ROY G. BIV and yesterday I learned a valuable lesson.

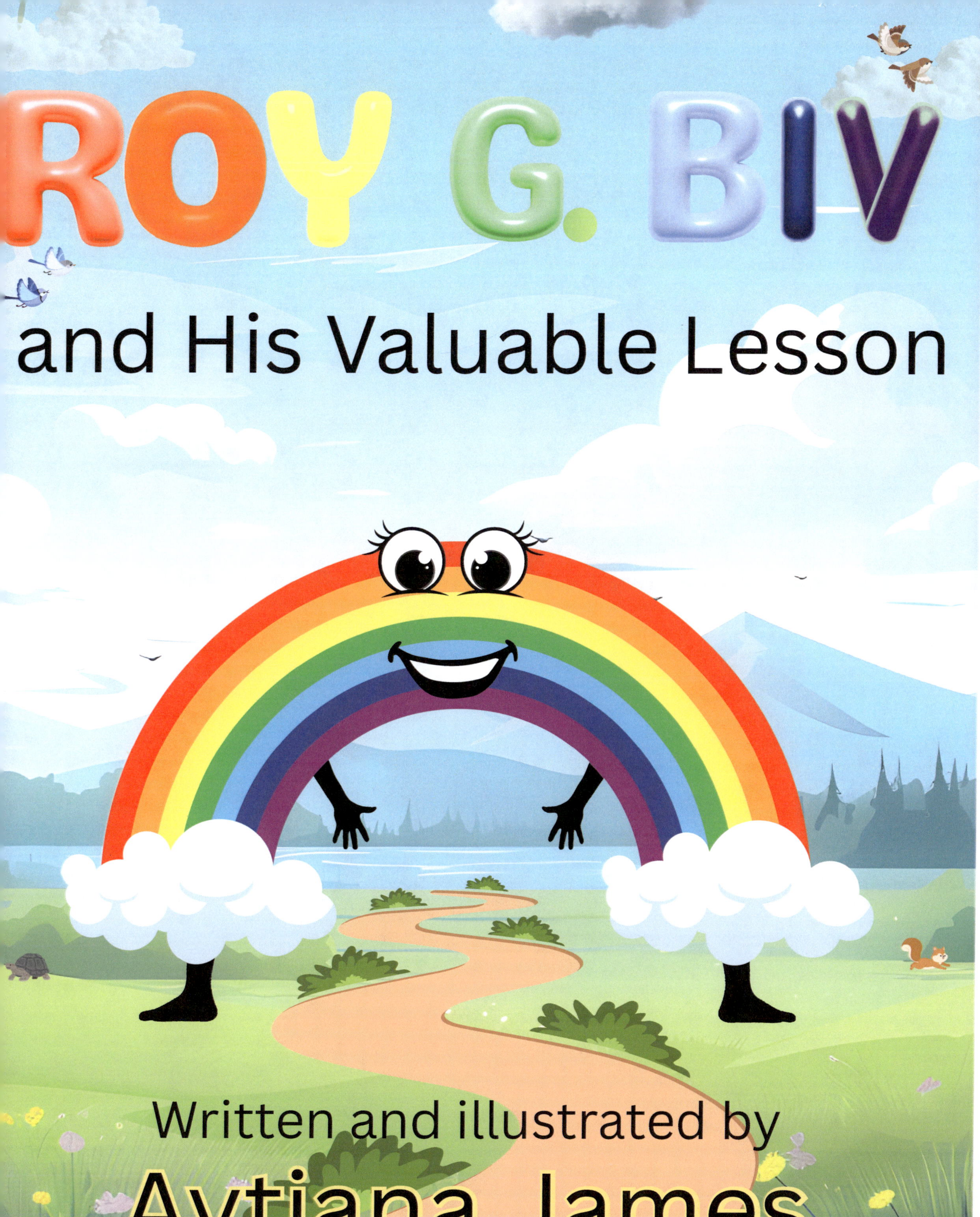

ROY G. BIV
and His Valuable Lesson
Written and illustrated by
Aytiana James

ROY G. BIV

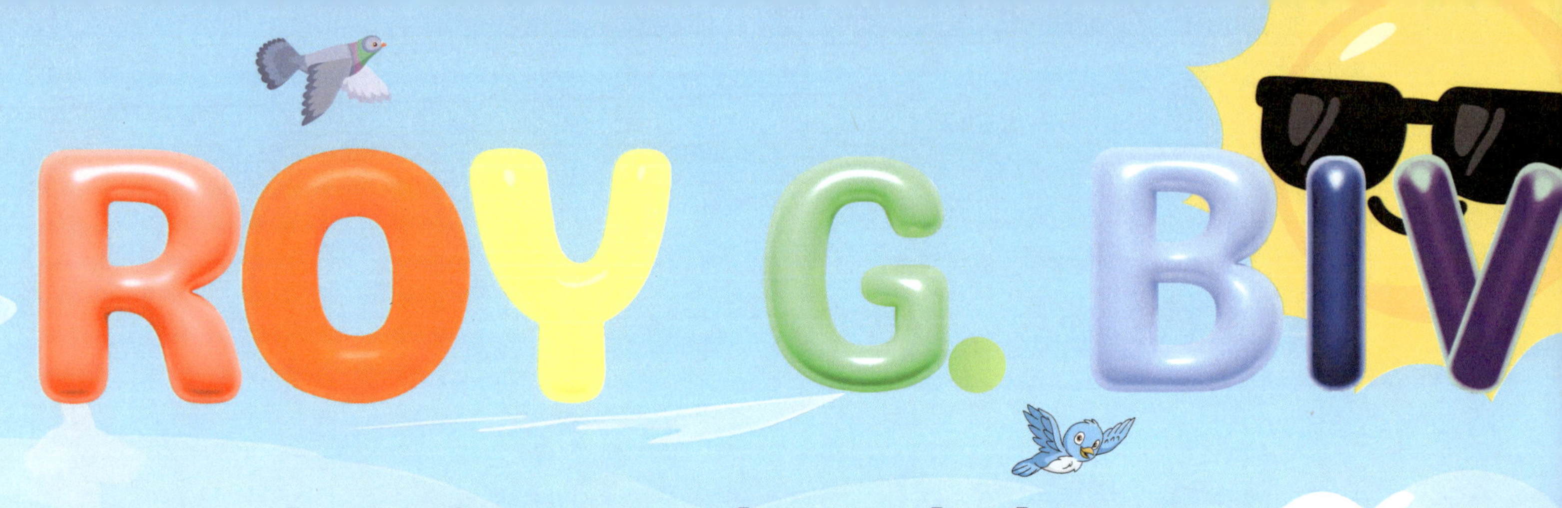

And His Valuable Lesson

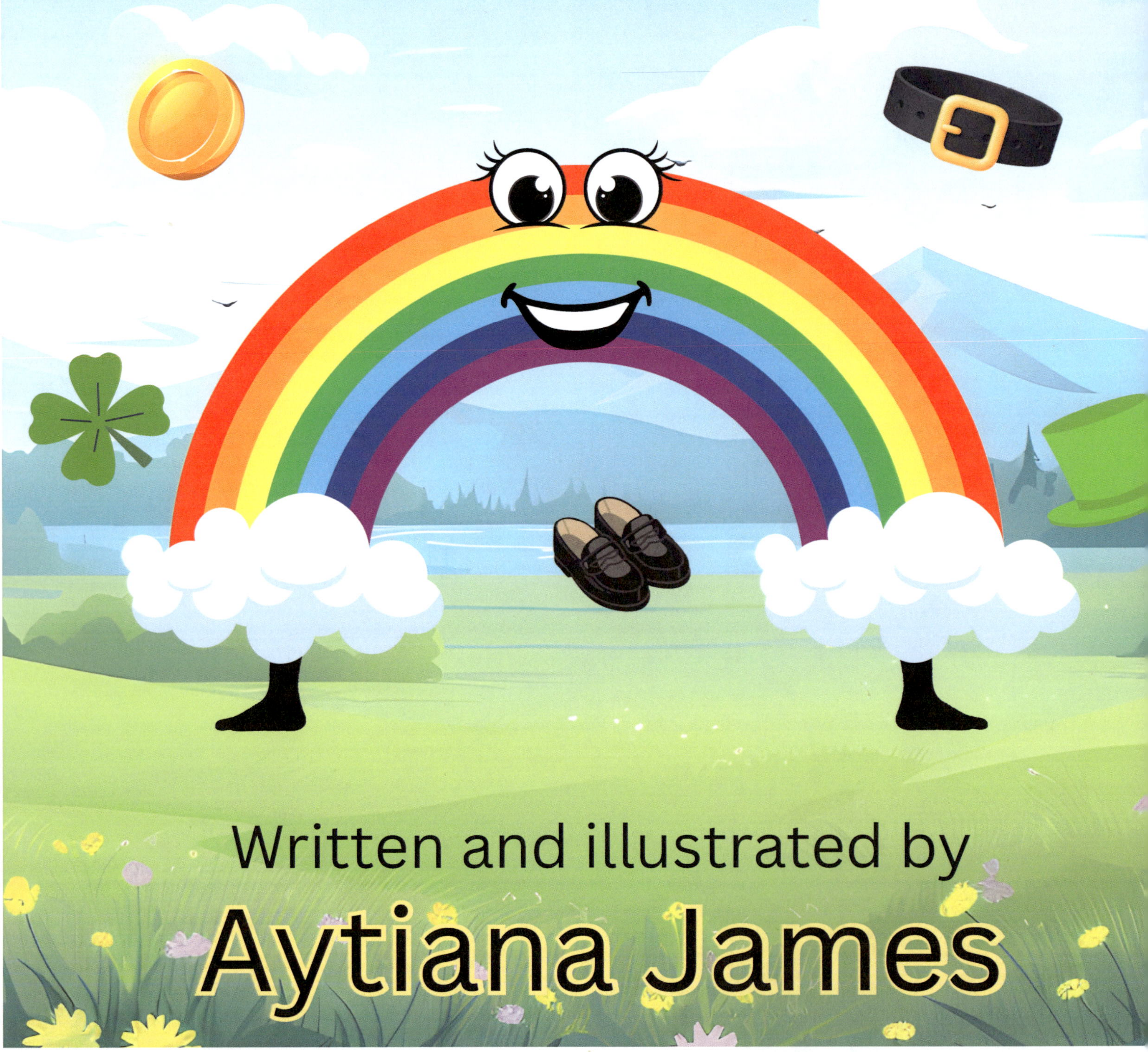

Written and illustrated by

Aytiana James

You see, it all started one morning when I was just minding my own business in the sky until I saw a shiny gold coin on the ground.

Now, at this point, I did what any rainbow would do. I jumped down to the ground and picked up the coin to put it in my cloud. However, at the time, I didn't notice that the red in my rainbow had vanished.

I was just too focused on looking up and deciding it was a beautiful day for a nature walk, so I began my stroll, singing a song.

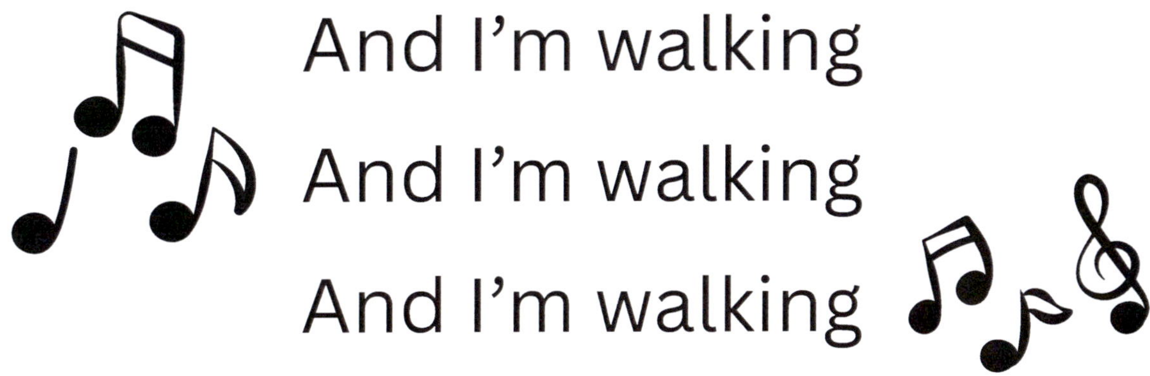

Ouuuu, it's my lucky day! There on the ground was a black belt with a solid gold buckle, so I did what any rainbow would do. I picked it up and put it in my cloud. However, at the time, I didn't notice that the orange in my rainbow had vanished.

I just continued my stroll while singing a song

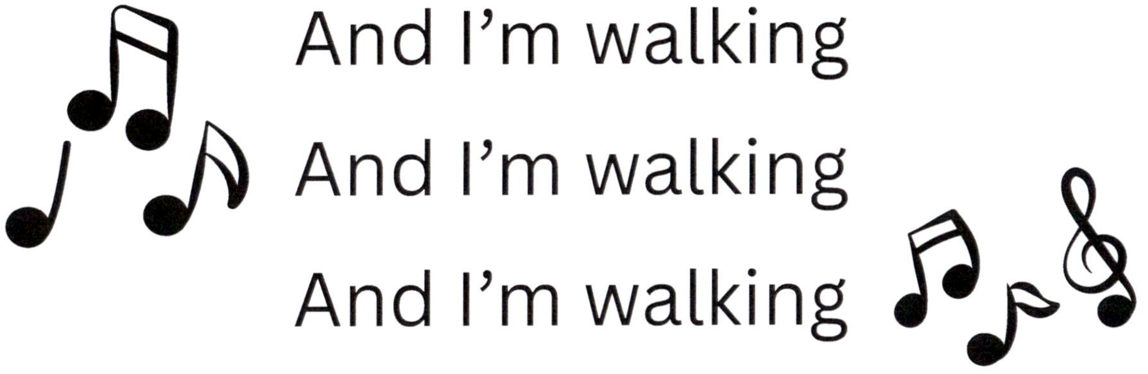

Ouuuu, I must be the luckiest rainbow in the world. There on the ground was a freshly polished green hat, so I did what any rainbow would do. I picked it up and put it in my cloud. However, at the time, I didn't notice that the yellow in my rainbow had vanished as well.

I just continued my stroll while singing a song

And I'm walking

And I'm walking

And I'm walking

Wait, what do we have here? In the middle of the path sat two shiny black shoes, so of course I did what any rainbow would do. I picked them up and put the fresh pair in my cloud. However, at the time I didn't notice that the green and blue in my rainbow had vanished.

I just continued my stroll while singing a song

And I'm walking
And I'm walking
And I'm walking 

Now that's just pure luck. Right there, perfectly still on the ground, was a four-leaf clover, so as you already know, I did what any rainbow would do. I picked it up and put it in my cloud. However, at the time, I didn't notice that the indigo in my rainbow had also vanished.

Now, at this point, I know exactly what you're thinking. He should have noticed his missing colors by now. Well, the fact is, I was just too happy. Besides, violet is the smallest color that I have. But anyway, I just continued my stroll, about to sing my song.

Suddenly, I heard the sound of crying nearby, so I decided to go see what was up. I soon discovered it was a tiny weeping man sitting on a black pot. Me of course, being me, I had to ask what was the matter.

The leprechaun stuttered and then spoke clearly, "An awful day it is, you see. A strong wind came and blew at me. My gold and things all flew away, and now I'm blue with dismay."

ROY G. BIV was concerned, but still, all he said was, "That sounds awful. I'm sorry I can't help you, but I do hope you find it." It was then that the violet vanished from the rainbow.

It was then that Roy turned to walk away, but caught his own reflection in the puddle of tears. At that point, the leprechaun wasn't the only one crying. Roy had finally realized all of his beautiful colors were grey. Seeing this, he knew exactly how the leprechaun felt, so he decided to do what was right.

One by one Roy took everything out of his cloud and handed it back.

Leprechaun: You found it! You found it! Thank you!

Roy: No thanks needed. I should have given it back when I first realized.

Leprechaun: Awww shucks you did the right thing in the end and that's what matters most.

Roy began to smile, feeling better than he had the entire day. Then that's when the magic happened: Roy got all seven of his colors back, brighter than ever. Happy as can be, Roy jumped back into the sky, knowing that he had learned a valuable lesson.

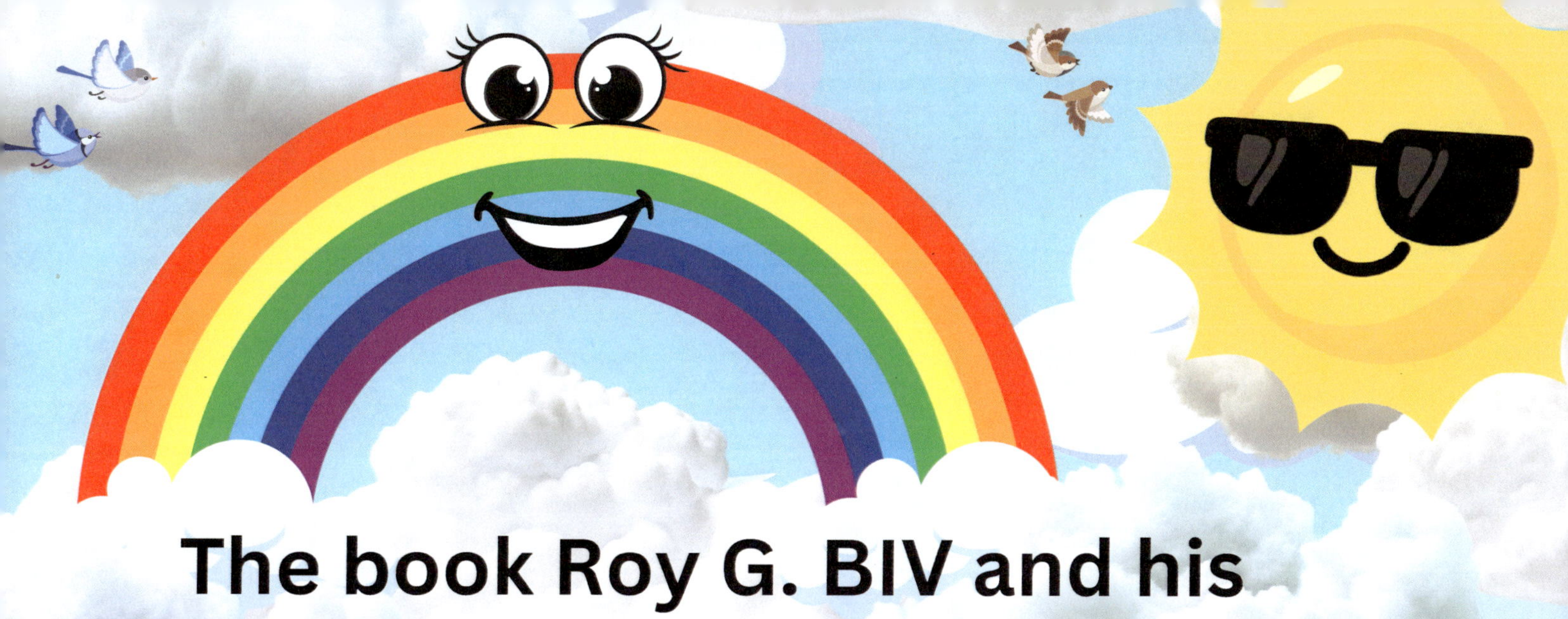

The book Roy G. BIV and his valuable lesson is a story about a rainbow, oblivious to his actions until he realizes the consequences and tries to make things right.

ROY G. BIV

Red
Orange
Yellow
Green
Blue
Indigo
Violet

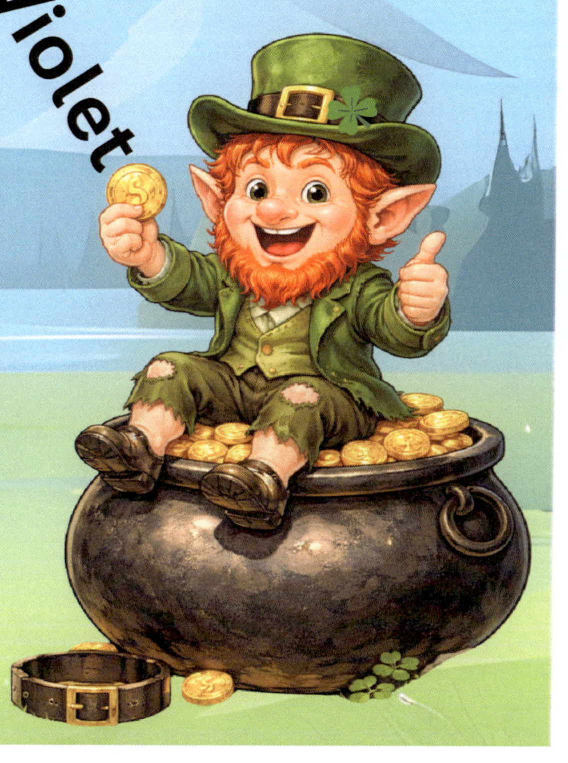

AJ'S CREATIONS

9 798234 061386